Hairy Bear

by Joy Cowley

Hairy Bear,
Hairy Bear,
I can hear robbers.

2

I don't care,
I don't care,
I'll fim-fam-fight 'em.

Hairy Bear,
Hairy Bear,
I can still hear robbers.

I don't care,
I don't care,
I'll bim-bam-bash 'em.

Hairy Bear,
Hairy Bear,
I'm frightened
of the robbers.

I don't care,
I don't care,
I'll crim-cram-crash 'em.

Hairy Bear,
Hairy Bear,

they might get
all our money.

I don't care,
I don't care,
I'll zim-zam-zap 'em.

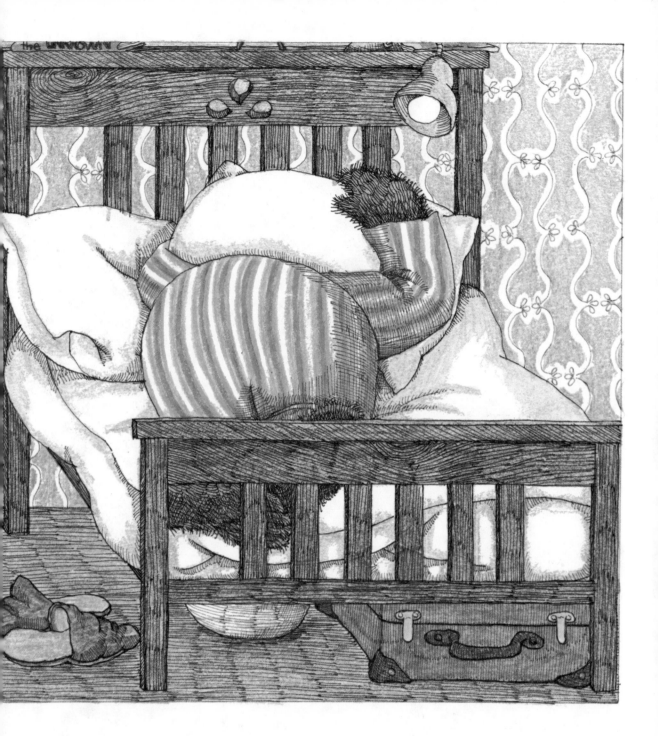

And I'll do it
in the morning.

Hairy Bear,
Hairy Bear,

you're just a
scaredy bear.

I'm **not** a scaredy bear.

I'm a brave and
dare-y bear.